Buffy the Vampire Slayer™

Note from the Underground

PAUL LEE *and* BRIAN HORTON

Buffy the Vampire Slayer™

Note from the Underground

based on the television series created by
JOSS WHEDON

writers SCOTT LOBDELL & FABIAN NICIEZA

penciller CLIFF RICHARDS

inker WILL CONRAD

colorist DAVE MCCAIG

letterer CLEM ROBINS

cover art PAUL LEE & BRIAN HORTON

This story takes place after Buffy the Vampire Slayer's sixth season.

DARK HORSE COMICS®

publisher
MIKE RICHARDSON

editor
SCOTT ALLIE
with MATT DRYER

designer
LANI SCHREIBSTEIN

art director
MARK COX

special thanks to
DEBBIE OLSHAN AT FOX LICENSING
AND DAVID CAMPITI AT GLASS HOUSE GRAPHICS

PUBLISHED BY
DARK HORSE COMICS, INC.
10956 SE MAIN STREET
MILWAUKIE, OR 97222

FIRST EDITION
MARCH 2003
ISBN: 1-56971-888-1

1 3 5 7 9 10 8 6 4 2

PRINTED IN CHINA

INTRODUCTION

With *Buffy* #50 approaching, I wanted a story bigger than anything we'd done before. *Blood of Carthage*, which climaxed in issue #25, had long been a favorite of mine, and it was time to outdo it. The loss of Tom Fassbender and Jim Pascoe as writers on the monthly was a real setback, but I'd already been talking to Scott Lobdell about doing some work on the title. When he signed on to pick up with issue #47, I figured my problems were solved.

I'd already gotten the idea to start the series over at #51, to go back to Buffy's roots (see *Buffy* #51 to #54, or the collection *Viva Las Buffy*, for details). So it seemed appropriate to bring back some old faces to wrap things up. Some people have suggested that Angel and Faith's inclusion in the book was a marketing ploy on Lobdell's part, but it was my idea, and it was meant to give the book a sense of closure. This is also the reason that San Sui, from *Buffy* #1 (*The Remaining Sunlight*) returned from the dustbin, as well as a score of other more or less familiar faces.

Fabian Nicieza, who'd contributed to *The Death of Buffy* story, jumped on to help Scott, adding his unique twist and his understanding of the characters, having an increasing influence through the course of the story. Cover artists Paul and Brian impressed readers with the little details linking covers #47 and #48 (see the cover to this volume and page 2), and they made their editor jump with joy at the Rockwell tributes for the two covers to issue #50 (these pages).

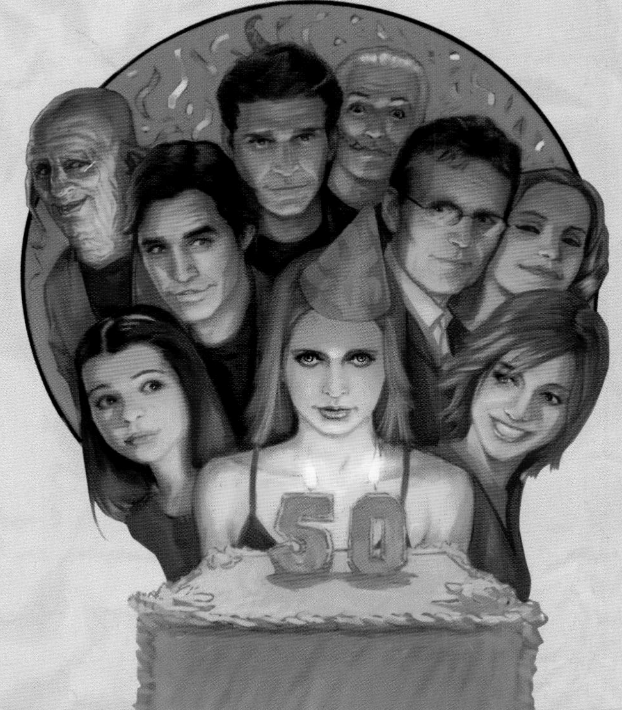

When Lobdell first talked to me about taking over the *Buffy* series, he said, "I think the best reason to do a *Buffy* comic is budget, budget, budget. By that I mean, everyone wants to see a feature version of *Buffy* because they know the budget will be big to really show Sunnydale, to really show Buffy and the Scooby Gang fighting a legion of the Damned, an Army of the Undead."

Perhaps that's all the intro *Note from the Underground* needs. We're celebrating the characters, celebrating the world Joss created, and opening things up a bit. Thanks for giving us the opportunity. Thanks for reading.

Scott Allie
Portland, Oregon

THE SUNNYDALE EVENING POST

TOK YHECHT MROHUME?
KRE USK FROE BELSAN.
STEGLAR FUSTRUPTUR ASACKOMC.
hee hee
OH, MUGS... I GET SO *HOT* WHEN YOUSE TALK ALL RUSSIAN LIKE THAT.
THE LANGUAGE ISN'T RUSSIAN --IT'S CH'UHNSKRIT.
THE WORDS WERE OLD WHEN ATLANTIS WAS STILL BEACH-FRONT PROPERTY.
THAT'S ONE THING ABOUT NIGHTLIFE HERE IN LOS ANGELES.
KNOW THE RIGHT PLACES?
DARE TO KNOCK ON THE RIGHT DOORS?
YOU CAN PRETTY MUCH FIND ANY-THING.

DANTE'S INFERNO IS A PERFECT EXAMPLE.
HIDDEN BEHIND AN ABANDONED STRIP MALL OFF LaCIENEGA, IT'S AN AFTERHOURS CLUB SERVING A CLIENTELE WITH A TASTE FOR DEMONIC DEGREDATION.
USTREK, FRON STEGLAR--
ENGLISH ALREADY, YA MUG. WHERE ARE YER MANNERS?

APOLOGIES, I.
WE SAID, "WELCOME. MR. STEGLAR EXPECTS MEETING YOU."
WOW.
NICE PLACE.

WAY HERE.
ANGEL THOSE POOR WOMEN...?
DAEMON EROTICUS--THEY LIVE OFF THE SEXUAL ENERGY OF HUMANS.
BUT...THE CHAINS?
THEY MUST BE VICTIMS OF A SLAVE-TRADE RING. WE'LL INVESTIGATE AFTER WE DO WHAT WE CAME HERE TO DO, CORDELIA. FOCUS.
CURIOUSLY, GIRL?
MAYBE FILL APPLICATION FOR EMPLOYMENT--HEH HEH.
UMMM... NOT THANKS.

EEEEP!
WH-WHAT HAPPENED TO YOUR HEAD?
"WH-WHAT HAPPENED TO YOUR HEAD? WH-WHAT HAPPENED TO YOUR HEAD?"
DO YOU REALIZE HOW MANY TIMES I'VE HEARD THAT OVER THE PAST CENTURY AND A HALF?
SIGH
I'M TELLING YOU... MUGSY, ISN'T IT? IF YOU DIDN'T COME SO HIGHLY RECOMMENDED FROM BELSAN, I WOULDN'T BE DEALING WITH YOU HUMANS AT ALL.
I DIDN'T COME ALL THIS WAY TO TRADE INSULTS WITH A DEMON TOO STUPID TO KEEP TRACK OF HIS OWN HEAD.
THIS IS ABOUT BUSINESS, STEGLAR. LET'S KEEP THE SMALL TALK TO SPORTS AND WEATHER.
I KNOW WHERE MY--
go dodgers?
HA HA--I LIKE YOUR STYLE, MUGSY. YOU GOT BITE.
I CAN SEE NOW WHY THAT LITTLE PHARMACOLOGICAL DEPENDANT BELSAN WAS SO ADAMANT THAT I TAKE THIS MEETING.
GENTLEMEN, GET THE MERCHANDISE.
YES, SIR.

TELL ME, MUGSY. WHAT DO YOU KNOW ABOUT SOUL DROPS?
PRETTY MUCH WHAT EVERYBODY ELSE KNOWS ABOUT 'EM.
IT'S BEEN CALLED THE DEVIL'S CANDY.
A DRUG WHAT GETS YA HIGH--
--THEN SLAMS YA LOWER THAN THE THIRD RING OF HELL.
I KNOW IT'S AS ADDICTIVE AS SIN ON A SATURDAY NIGHT.
THAT ONCE A PERSON'S HOOKED, YA'D GIVE UP YER SOUL FOR ANOTHER HIT.
YER SOUL, OR ANYONE ELSE'S YA CAN GET YER HANDS ON.
I KNOW IT'S ILLEGAL IN PRETTY MUCH EVERY DIMENSION I CAN THINK OF. POSSESSION ALONE IS PUNISHABLE BY ETERNAL TORMENT.
MUGSY HONEY-- JUST LOOKING AT IT GIVES ME THE CHILLS. WH--WHAT IS IT?
SOUL DROPS.
IT'S A DRUG HARVESTED FROM THE SOULS OF THE UNBORN.
EW.

DON'T YOU WANT TO SAMPLE THE MERCHANDISE?
OH, TAKE A FEW. THEY'RE ON THE HOUSE.
I'M A RETAILER, NOT A CONSUMER.
BUT I NEED TO KNOW WHERE YOU'RE GETTING YER SUPPLY.
SO YOU CAN CUT ME OUT?
NOT HARDLY. SO I KNOW YA AIN'T GONNA LEAVE ME HOLDIN' AN EMPTY BAG WHEN DROPPERS KEEP COMIN' BACK AFTER THEY'RE HOOKED.
NEVER!
THEN FORGET IT.
MUGSY, CALM DOWN. DON'T BE SO RASH.
I CAN TELL YOU THIS MUCH--THE SOUL DROPS ARE FRESH. SHIPPED DAILY...
...STRAIGHT FROM THE HELLMOUTH.
THE...HELL-MOUTH?
YES. YOU EVER HEAR OF A PLACE CALLED... SUNNYDALE?
...

VISIONS.
SUDDEN, VIOLENT, GRAPHIC...THEY HAVE PLAGUED CORDELIA CHASE SINCE SHE WAS BEQUEATHED THEM BY THE POWERS THAT BE.
RECENTLY SHE'S COME TO SUSPECT IT WAS ALL PART OF A BIGGER PLAN.
NOT THAT THEY HURT ANY LESS.
CORDELIA, WHAT?!
IF I HAVEN'T SAID IT RECENTLY...?
OW!
THUK
THUNK

YOU OKAY?
UMM... MOSTLY.
BUT I GUESS I BLEW OUR COVER.
I'LL SAY! WHO BRINGS WOODEN STAKES TO A BUSINESS MEETING?
DEVOUR THEM AT WILL, GENTLE-MEN.
SORRY, GUYS, THE KITCHEN'S CLOSED FOR THE EVENING.
YOU'RE A VAMPIRE TOO?!
VAMPIRE WITH A SOUL?
EVERY-ONE HEARD OF THE TRAITOR ANGELUS!
YEAH, WELL --MOST PEOPLE JUST ASK FOR AN AUTOGRAPH.
CRUNCH
THAT'S IT! GET HIM WHILE HE'S DOWN!
TOO BAD FOR YOU, "ANGEL"--NOT A STAKE IN SIGHT!
WHAT ARE YOU DOING?!
I'LL REFRAIN FROM THE OBVIOUS "JUST TRYING TO GET AHEAD" JOKE.

IT'S THE SOUL.
IT THROWS EVERYONE OFF.
THUK!
THAK!
ARRRRGH!
YEAH, I KNOW. IT WAS EITHER THAT OR "HEAD'S UP."
THIS IS HUMILIATING!

IF YOU'RE TRYING TO RIP ME OFF--MY LAWYERS WILL HAVE YOUR SOUL. HAVE YOU EVER HEARD OF WOLFRAM AND HART?!
CORDY, ARE YOU OKAY?
ANGEL...
THE VISION? SOME-ONE'S IN TROUBLE, DEEP.
FINE, WE'LL FIGURE OUT HOW TO--
ANGEL... IT'S BUFFY.
LET'S GO. BUT FIRST--
YOU'VE DESTROYED ALL THOSE SOULS?!
FWOOSH
NO. I'VE RELEASED THEM.
Y-YOU'LL NEVER GET AWAY WITH THIS!
I JUST DID.
THIS IS GOING TO HURT!

LIKE ANY GREAT CITY, LOS ANGELES HAS ITS MANY SIDES.
FOR EVERY DEMONIC STRIP JOINT--
--THERE'S A QUIET HOUSE IN BEVERLY HILLS.
THE HOME OF JUDGE MARGET BROWN.
YOU LITTLE ANGEL. EVERY NIGHT I THANK GOD FOR BRINGING YOU TO ME.
THAT'S NOT THE WAY I REMEMBER IT HAPPENING.
WHAT--?!
INVITE ME IN, MARGET.
WE HAVE TO TALK.

SOON.
YOU REALIZE IF ANYTHING GOES WRONG WITH THIS PLAN OF YOURS, IT WILL COST ME THE BENCH?
I COULD EVEN GET THROWN INTO PRISON MYSELF.
I REALIZE I'M ASKING A LOT.
I'M SORRY.
I'LL FIND ANOTHER WAY.
YOU'LL DO NO SUCH THING.
WHEN MY DAUGHTER GOT INVOLVED WITH THAT PANGEAN ORGAN BLACK MARKET--
--WHEN SHE SOLD THEM HER OWN DAUGHTER TO PAY FOR HER ADDICTION--
--YOU WERE THE ONLY ONE I COULD TURN TO.
ANGEL INVESTIGATIONS WAS THE ONLY PLACE THAT COULD HELP.
I WOULDN'T EVEN HAVE MY GRANDDAUGHTER IF IT WEREN'T FOR YOU, ANGEL.
HELLO, IT'S ME.
WAKE THE GOVERNOR.

NEVER A BIG FAN OF SLEEP.
TOO VULNERABLE.
WHO NEEDS ALL THOSE SUBCONSCIOUS THOUGHTS ROILING UNFETTERED THROUGHOUT YOUR BRAIN PAN ALL NIGHT?
AND THAT WAS BEFORE SHE WAS CALLED.
BEFORE SHE WAS CHARGED BY THE WATCHER'S COUNCIL WITH THE ANCIENT VOCATION: SLAYER.
BEFORE THE MURDER OF AN INNOCENT MAN--AND THE CONSEQUENCES SHE ACCEPTED WHEN SHE TURNED HERSELF IN TO THE AUTHORITIES.
BEFORE HER FALL FROM GRACE.

...AND HER STRUGGLE FOR REDEMPTION.
!
IT'S BARELY A GASP.
FAITH HAS NEVER BEEN ONE FOR EXCLAMATIONS.
SHE'D RATHER KEEP IT TO HERSELF.
EVERY-THING'S COOL.
FIVE BY FIVE.
FAITH-- BAD DREAM AGAIN?
YEAH, OMEKA. SORRY TO WAKE YOU.
GO BACK TO SLEEP-- I'M FINE.
NO LUCKY
DOC LARA
WARREN'S A BITCH!
SON OF A
I ONLY SHARE THIS CELL A WEEK, FAITH. BUT YOU ARE NOT FINE.
LET ME TAKE YOU TO PRISON PSYCHOLOGIST.
HE HELP YOU TAME YOUR DEMONS.
THAT'S... ALMOST FUNNY.
SHARE, FAITH. TELL ME WHAT PAINS YOU--
FRONT AND CENTER, FAITH.

IF THIS IS ABOUT THE STAFF SLUMBER PARTY, FORGET IT.
LIKE I TOLD THE FIRST GUARD THAT TRIED IT, I DON'T SWING THAT WAY.
WATCH YOUR MOUTH, GIRL, OR YOU'RE GONNA FIND IT HARD TO SLEEP WITH A NIGHTSTICK SHOVED--
OFFICER BENSKI, PLEASE. YOU KNOW FAITH HERE IS ONE OF MY FAVORITE YOUNG CHARGES.
WHICH IS WHY IT IS SO PAINFUL FOR ME TO SAY GOOD BYE.
I'M... LEAVING?
FOR TWENTY-FOUR HOURS, APPARENTLY.
BUT THEN YOU'LL BE BACK, FAITH. AND YOU'LL BE ALL MINE.
I MIGHT BE BACK--
--BUT I'LL NEVER BE YOURS.
AND FOR THE HUNDREDTH TIME TODAY...
...SHE HAS TO REMIND HERSELF WHY SHE SUBJECTS HERSELF TO THIS.

THEY SAID I WAS REMANDED TO YOUR CUSTODY--FOR TWENTY-FOUR HOURS?
I'LL EXPLAIN ON THE WAY. I HAVE TO ASK YOU TO TRUST ME.
ALWAYS.

SOMEWHERE BETWEEN THE DRUG PARLORS AND THE JUDGE'S HOMES AND THE FEDERAL PRISONS...
...THERE ARE PLACES LIKE THE FORMER HYPERION HOTEL.
CURRENTLY THE HOME OF ANGEL INVESTIGATIONS.
MAYBE THE ONLY DETECTIVE AGENCY RUN BY A VAMPIRE WITH A SOUL IN SEARCH OF REDEMPTION.
A SEARCH THAT IS ALTERNATELY AIDED AND COMPLICATED BY THE GROUP HE'S ASSEMBLED SINCE HIS ARRIVAL IN THIS SOUTHERN CALIFORNIA CITY.
THIS IS CRAZY! YOU ARE OUT OF YOUR MIND IF YOU THINK WE'RE LETTING YOU GO THERE ALONE!
GUNN IS RIGHT, ANGEL. IF SOMETHING TOOK DOWN BUFFY ON HER OWN--MAYBE YOU'D BE DOING HER A FAVOR BY BRINGING HER MORE BACK-UP.
INSTEAD OF LESS.
YOU REALLY SHOULD LET US HELP.
IF ANGEL THINKS HE CAN HANDLE THIS, PRINCESS--IT IS NOT GROO'S PLACE TO ARGUE.

ENOUGH, PEOPLE. WE'RE BURNING MIDNIGHT HERE WHILE BUFFY'S IN WHO KNOWS WHAT KIND OF TROUBLE.
WE DON'T KNOW THAT FOR SURE. IT COULD HAVE BEEN ONE OF THOSE FUTURE VISION THINGIES.
SHE MAY BE FINE, FOR NOW.
WHAT IS THIS, A DEMOCRACY? I THOUGHT YOU GUYS WORKED FOR ANGEL--NOT THE OTHER WAY AROUND.
CORDELIA'S VISION SHOWED FAITH AND I ON OUR WAY TO HELP.
IT'S WHY I GOT HER OUT OF PRISON, AND IT'S WHY WE'RE GOING.
ALONE.
THAT'S A TOTAL STEAMING HEAP OF AN EXCUSE, ANGEL!
EITHER WE'RE IN THIS TOGETHER OR NOT AT ALL!
FAITH?!
STOP TELLING ANGEL WHAT TO DO--WHILE YOU STILL HAVE A TONGUE IN YOUR HEAD!
YOU THINK I'M SCARED OF YOU, HALF-PINT?
NO, YOU'RE PROBABLY TOO STUPID TO BE SCARED OF ME!
THIS ISN'T HELPING.
OH, I'M SORRY, "PRINCESS." I SUPPOSE WE CAN SIT ON OUR BUTTS UNTIL YOU HAVE ANOTHER SEIZURE. ANOTHER CRYPTIC DREAM SEQUENCE IS JUST THE THING WE NEED.
THERE'S NO ACCOUNT TO TALK TO THE PRINCESS THAT WAY!
SOME-TIMES IT WAS SO MUCH QUIETER IN PYLEA.

SOON...
NICE FRIENDS YOU HAVE THERE.
THEY'RE A GOOD BUNCH.
JUST A BIT ...WILLFUL.
MAKES ME THINK I SHOULD BAG THIS WHOLE "REDEMPTION" GIG IN JAIL.
FAITH...
DON'T WORRY, DON'T WORRY--I KNOW I'M GOING BACK WHEN ALL THIS IS OVER.
I'M JUST SAYING, LOOK AT YOU. YOU'VE GOT, WHAT--TWO HUNDRED-PLUS YEARS OF BLOODLETTING TO MAKE UP FOR?
MAYBE... MAYBE YOU WOULDN'T MIND SOME HELP, IS ALL I'M SAYING.
I MEAN, I AM A SLAYER.
SHOULDN'T I BE SLAYING?

SEVERAL HUNDRED MILES AWAY...
...IN A DARKENED CORNER OF THE CITY OF SUNNYDALE...
...BUFFY SUMMERS IS HAVING HER OWN DIFFICULTY CURRENTLY FULFILLING THE ROLE OF SLAYER.
UNLIKE FAITH, WHO WAS ALWAYS A LONER--
--BUFFY'S EARLY TEEN YEARS WERE THE STUFF OF ADOLESCENT ENVY.
CUTE BOYS, STYLISH CLOTHES, THE CHEERLEADING SQUAD, AND ONLY THE COOLEST OF FRIENDS.
THINGS HAVE GONE DECIDEDLY DOWNHILL SINCE THEN.

SHKINK
RILEY FINN

HOLD ON, BUFFY--
--HELP IS ON ITS WAY.

BUFFY SUMMERS. THE SLAYER. CHOSEN TO PROTECT THE INNOCENT FROM THE UGLY SHADOWS OF THE NIGHT.
BUT WHO PROTECTS THE SLAYER?
DEEP GASHES HEAL. A FRACTURED TIBIA MENDS.
ALL SO SHE CAN FIGHT... AGAIN.
AND AGAIN. AND AGAIN...
THE GOOD NEWS-- SHE'S STILL ALIVE.

THOUGH THAT HAPPENS TO BE THE BAD NEWS, TOO.
WORD SPREAD AROUND TOWN THAT A DEMON GLADIATOR RING HAD STARTED UP.
THEY TRACKED IT DOWN TO AN UNDERGROUND CHAMBER AT SUNNYDALE UNIVERSITY, FORMER OUTPOST OF THE COVERT GOVERNMENT ORGANIZATION CALLED THE INITIATIVE.

SHE'S BEATEN DOWN TWENTY-SIX CHALLENGERS IN FOUR DAYS.
SOON-TO-BE NUMBER TWENTY-SEVEN IS NAMED SAN SUI.
AN ANCIENT CHINESE VAMPIRE SHE'D DUSTED YEARS AGO...
HE SHOULD BE DEAD, BUT SHE CAN'T THINK ABOUT THAT.
PROCESSES THOUGHT INTO MOTION.
IT'S THE ONLY WAY SHE'LL SURVIVE.
AND SHE WILL SURVIVE...

...BECAUSE THEY NEED HER...
XANDER, CAN YOU SEE ANYTHING?
UHM... NEGATIVE, BUT I'M SURE SHE'S OKAY, DAWN.
YOU'LL SEE, SCRAPPY DOO, ANY MINUTE NOW--

--SHE'LL COME BARGING THROUGH THE WALL WITH COMPLETE DISREGARD FOR EVERY RULE *MISS MANNERS* LIVES BY--
--HACK A FEW DEMON HEADS OFF, AND RESCUE US.
YOU THINK?
I KNOW.

IS IT HER?
NO, BUT A CLOSE SECOND --TIME FOR SLOP...!
"...WILL WE BE HAVING ENTRAILS WITH TOENAILS, OR TOENAILS WITH ENTRAILS?"
"UGH. WHAT'S THE DIFFERENCE?"
"AH, TO YOUR ADOLESCENT PALETTE, NOTHING, BUT TO MY WORLDLY TONGUE.."
"YOU DID NOT JUST SAY..."
HEY, HEY! SINGLE FILE, KIDS! SIN-GULL-FILE!
DO NOT MAKE ME HAVE TO TURN THIS CELL AROUND AND GO HOME!
THINK HARD UNTIL YOUR BRAIN HURTS --REMEMBER YESTERDAY?
EVERY-ONE GETS A BOWL, ONE AT A TIME.
SO, ANYANKA, ANY-THING INTERESTING ON TODAY'S MENU?
IT IS STILL SLOP.

...
BECAUSE I THOUGHT, MAYBE, YOU'D HAVE A SURPRISE ...
AH, YES, I UNDER-STAND-- PRISON CODE.
I DID LEARN THIS IS A DRUG-THING.
THEY ARE EXTRACTING PAIN, MISERY, LOSS --ALL THE GOOD EMOTIONS--
--AND TURNING THEM INTO A POWER-FUL NARCOTIC CALLED SOUL DROPS.
BUT WE STILL NEED TO FIND OUT THE WHO-IS-DOING-IT AND THE WHERE-IS-IT-GOING.
I--I DO NOT KNOW THAT YET...
NO ONE WILL TALK TO ME WHEN I LOOK LIKE THIS.
PEOPLE GET VERY AGITATED WHEN THEY ARE TOO CLOSE TO A VENGEANCE DEMON, YOU KNOW.

CAN YOU BLAME THEM?
NO, AHN. I WAS SAYING--
OH, NOW THIS TURNS INTO HOW COULD I LOVE ANYA, THE DEMON--
--HOW COULD SOMEONE NOT GET WORKED UP AROUND YOU? MY HEART'S ABOUT TO BURST...
OH. I--AHA--HMM...
LET'S MOVE IT.
WE'LL BE OKAY. TRY TO HELP BUFFY IF YOU CAN...
...AND STAY SAFE...
YOU SO STILL LOVE HER!

"WHAT'S GOING ON NOW?"
"WILD GUESS-- MORE FIGHTING."
XANDER HARRIS DOESN'T TELL DAWN THE TRUTH.
HE RECOGNIZES THE FISTS OF FURY THEATER REJECT, BUT HE'S NOT SURE FROM WHERE.
AFTER A WHILE, THE DEMONS THEY FOUGHT HAD ALL STARTED LOOKING ALIKE.
HE TOOK THEM FOR GRANTED...
...JUST LIKE HE TOOK SOMETHING ELSE FOR GRANTED--
--THAT BUFFY WOULD ALWAYS WIN!

THEN AGAIN...
XANDER CAN TELL SOMETHING IS WRONG.
THERE'S SOMETHING ABOUT HER...
...THEY'D RARELY SEEN IT, ALWAYS TALKED ABOUT IT--
WHAT WOULD HAPPEN IF BUFFY GAVE IN TO IT?
SURRENDERED HERSELF TO HER POWERS? HER ANGER?

WHAT IF SHE STOPPED BEING BUFFY--
--AND JUST BECAME THE SLAYER?

MEANWHILE, AT THE STORE FORMERLY KNOWN AS THE MAGIC BOX...
RETAIL SUCKS.
WHATEVER HAPPENED HERE, FAITH... IT WAS BAD.
SO THE STRINGS YOU PULLED TO GET ME A "WEEKEND PASS" FROM JAIL WAS FOR NOTHING?
I DON'T KNOW...
I CAN MARK SCENTS FROM THE DRIED BLOOD--
--MORE THAN ONE PERSON, A MIX OF MEN AND WOMEN...
PROBABLY ALL MY BEST BUDDIES. DID THEY DIE HERE?
NO. BUT THEY FOUGHT HERE.
ABOUT TWO WEEKS AGO.
AND ANGEL, THE VAMPIRE WITH A SOUL, DIDN'T COME BACK TO HELP POOR BUFFY, THE LOVE OF HIS LIFE?
I'VE BEEN DEALING WITH MY OWN PROBLEMS.
SO, WHERE ARE THEY NOW?
I'M TRYING TO TRACK THEIR SCENTS, BUT THE TRAIL IS COLD.

"BUFFY IS LOST..."

BUDDA
BUDDA
BUDDA
"WAS THAT GUNFIRE?"

IS BUFFY OKAY?
YES.
WHO WAS SHOOTING A GUN?
WELL, IT'S NOT COMMANDER XANDER WITH THE KUNG-FU GRIP, BUT IT'S THE NEXT BEST THING--
--OUR FAVORITE SUPER-SOLDIER, AND I DON'T MEAN CAPTAIN AMERICA!
NO MATTER WHAT... DO NOT WET YOUR PANTS...

GYAAAAA!!!

HI, BUFFY. LONG TIME, NO SEE...
HANG ON TIGHT!
OR JUST BEHEAD AWAY...
...YOUR CALL ON THAT ONE...

SHE FEELS THE LEATHER. SMELLS THE SCENT ON HIS CLOTHES. FAMILIAR. SAFE.
SLOWLY, SHE IS DRAWN BACK...
...TO HUMANITY...
314
TO A WORLD THAT ISN'T AS "EASY" AS KILL OR BE KILLED.
A COMPLICATED WORLD MADE UP OF VERY...
...COMPLICATED PEOPLE...?
MAGGIE WALSH.
SHE RAN THE INITIATIVE, A GROUP OF SOLDIER BOYS WHO USED THIS CHAMBER TO CAGE DEMONS--
--SO GOVERNMENT MAD SCIENTISTS COULD STUDY THEM.
BUT THEY BROKE THE PLACE UP-- AND WALSH DIED.
BUT SO HAD SAN SUI.
AND HADN'T BUFFY DIED, TOO?
TWICE.

COMPLICATIONS. SHE SQUEEZES HER EYES SHUT.
SHE NEEDS TO KEEP THINGS SIMPLE WHILE COMING DOWN FROM THE BLOODLUST.
WELCOME
to
SUNNYDALE
Enjoy your stay!

FFTT-- UHM
SORRY ABOUT MY HAND THERE--
--WELL, NOT REALLY--
BUFFY--? YOU OKAY?

NO!
I DIDN'T ASK TO BE RESCUED!
WAIT, YOU CAN'T GO BACK TO THAT PLACE--
MY FRIENDS ARE STILL THERE.
MY SISTER!
YOU'RE HURT-- EXHAUSTED-- YOU CAN'T BEAT THEM ALL--
I'M THE SLAYER!

STUBBORN.
RECKLESS.
FEARLESS.
YOU HAVEN'T CHANGED A BIT.
ALL RIGHT. LET'S DO IT.
SAY AGAIN?
YOU MIGHT'VE FORGOTTEN--
--BUT I SAID I'D ALWAYS HAVE YOUR BACK.
RILEY FINN
THANKS, RILEY.
HUH? OH, THIS? YOU ACTUALLY KNOW THIS RILEY FINN GUY?
I JUST SCARFED HIS CLOTHES TO DO THE EVEL KNIEVEL THING.
BUFFY, IT'S ME--

PIKE!

BUFFY? HELLO?
UHM... ANYONE HOME?
NOT QUITE THE REUNION HE EXPECTED.
PIKE KNEW BUFFY WHEN SHE FIRST BECAME THE SLAYER.
--CHOSEN TO PROTECT INNOCENTS FROM THINGS THAT GO BUMP IN THE NIGHT.
THINGS HAPPENED, SHE MOVED OUT OF LOS ANGELES ...YADDA, YADDA...
TWENTY MINUTES AGO HE RESCUED BUFFY FROM AN UNDERGROUND DEMON ARENA OF DOOM.
AND THAT'S ONLY BEEN THE SECOND WEIRDEST PART OF THE NIGHT...

WATCHING BUFFY GO FROM YOSEMITE SAM TO DAN QUAYLE...
...WITH NO CLUE WHY--
...WELL, THAT WAS WEIRD!
BUFFY--C'MON--ARE YOU SORT OF MEDITATING?
'CAUSE THE LEAST YOU COULD DO IS CLOSE YOUR EYES--
OKAY.
S'COOL. WE WAIT.
YOU HAVE TO VEG A BIT, YOU DO IT...

--YOU ARE FREAKING ME OUT HERE...
BUFFY--?
...I GOT YOUR BACK.
AND THIS TIME...
CHIK-KLIK
...I'M NOT RUNNING AWAY.

uhm...IS THIS, LIKE, A SLAYER INTERVENTION ?
WE NEED TA BE SHOWIN' YOU SOMET'IN, BUFFY.
I SORT OF GOT THAT, KENDRA--
BUT IN CASE YOU HAVEN'T NOTICED--
--WHICH, WHAT WITH ALL OF YOU BEING DEAD AND IN MY HEAD, I'M TOTALLY GETTING THAT YOU HAVEN'T--
--BUT RIGHT NOW MIGHT NOT BE THE BEST TIME FOR SLAYER 101.

OKAY, SLURPEE HEAD-ACHE...
E! CELEBRITY PROFILE UNREELING IN MY--IN OUR HEADS? AND I GET TO NARRATE?
THERE'S ME IN L.A. POPULAR CHEER-LEADER BY DAY--
--VAMPIRE SLAYER BY NIGHT.
PIKE HELPED ME ASH A NEST OF VAMPS, BURNED THE SCHOOL GYM DOWN--
--WENT ON A ROAD TRIP TO VEGAS--
--GOT KICKED OUT OF SCHOOL--
--AND FROM THERE TO A COMFY BED FOR THE "EMOTIONALLY EXHAUSTED."
PARENTS FINALLY DID THE "D." 50/50 BY LAW --MOM GOT THE KIDS, HE GOT A LIFE.
AND WE GOT A NEW START IN SUNNY-DALE.

A TOWN WHICH MY NEW WATCHER, GILES, WAS NICE ENOUGH TO TELL ME, JUST HAPPENED TO BE THE HELLMOUTH, TOILET BOWL FOR ALL DEMON DOODY.
MIGHT'VE RUN BACK TO THE ASYLUM THEN AND THERE IF IT WEREN'T FOR THE FRIENDS I MADE--WILLOW, XANDER, OZ, CORDELIA--
I HAD TO KILL HIM BECAUSE OF IT, BUT EVENTUALLY, HE FORGAVE ME. LONG STORY. BUY THE DVD.
AFTER HE CAME BACK FROM A FEW THOUSAND YEARS IN HELL, HE NEEDED TO FEEL EVEN WORSE ABOUT HIMSELF-- SO HE MOVED TO L.A.
JOKE THERE, 'KAY?
SO I JUMPED OFF A BRIDGE.
STILL WITH THE JOKES.
I SACRIFICED MY LIFE TO SAVE THE WORLD...AND MORE IMPORTANTLY, MY SISTER.
BUT MY FRIENDS COULDN'T LEAVE DEAD ENOUGH ALONE, SO THEY YANKED ME OUT OF HEAVEN AND BACK INTO HELLMOUTH.
ANNE SUMMERS

...AND, OH YEAH, ANGEL, LOVE OF MY LIFE--
--WHO HAPPENED TO BE A VAMPIRE WITH A SOUL--
--AND A GYPSY CURSE THAT MADE HIM LOSE THAT SOUL AFTER WE--
--uhm-- LET'S JUST SAY IT WAS A MEMORABLE FIRST TIME.
LIFE GOES ON. COLLEGE --NEW BOYFRIEND--
--WHO HAPPENS TO BE SOLDIER STUD FOR AN ARMY DEMON-HUNTING SQUAD.
THAT ONE DIDN'T WORK OUT EITHER.
BEEN A ROUGH YEAR. DID THINGS... I'M NOT PROUD OF...
...BUT I'M KEEPIN' ON KEEPIN' ON, RIGHT?
SO YOU JUST RAN ME THROUGH A CLIFF NOTES VERSION OF MY LIFE--

"--NOW WHAT?"
DAWN!
MOVE, MEAT!
XANDER!
DAWN-- DON'T!
FEISTY MEAT!
I TOLD YOU TO STAY BEHIND!
I'M A TEENAGER, IT'S ILLEGAL FOR ME TO LISTEN TO YOU.
BEEN THERE, DONE THAT. BUT THIS COULD BE DANGEROUS--
AS OPPOSED TO BEING PICKED OUT OF THE CROWD TO FIGHT IN THE ARENA?
SCORING POINTS. OKAY, BUT WE DON'T KNOW WHERE THEY'RE TAKING US--
--AND WITH BUFFY GONE...

THERE'S ALL THE MORE REASON WE SHOULD STICK TOGETHER.
HUH?
ANYA? WHAT ARE YOU DOING HERE?
YOU WERE OUR INSIDE TRACK TO FIGURE OUT WHAT'S GOING ON.
I DROPPED MY DEMON-FORM FOR A SECOND-- BECAUSE IT REALLY MAKES MY FORE-HEAD ITCH--
--AND THE SCOURGE SAW ME--AND WELL, THEY DON'T LIKE HUMANS-- OR SUB-HUMANS... OR HALF-HUMANS --OR ANYTHING WITH THE WORD HUMAN IN IT-- VERY MUCH.
SO NOW YOU'RE STUCK HERE.
YES.
COULD BE WORSE, RIGHT?
I COULD BE MARCHING TO MY DEATH ALONGSIDE THE MAN WHO LEFT ME AT THE ALTAR!
Uhm... YOU ARE.
WELL THEN, THAT ANSWERS THAT...

"...OR WAS THAT TOO IRONICALLY SUBTLE FOR YOU?"
OW.
MY LIFE, MY MEMORIES--NO ROCK UPSIDE THE HEAD!
THEN AGAIN, MAYBE THE SMACK LED TO A CONCUSSION WHICH LED TO AMNESIA...
...BECAUSE I DEFINITELY WOULD'VE REMEMBERED FLINTSTONES BY WAY OF VAN GOGH.
SEE, MOM, SOMETIMES I WAS PAYING ATTENTION...

OKAY, FANCY MASKS AND TAMMY FAE MAKEUP IS SPOOKY, SURE--
--BUT THEY'RE NOT LOOKING AT ME LIKE I'M THE *PREY*...
...THEY THINK I'M THE *PREDATOR*?
SURE, WHITE FACE, BLONDE HAIR, ALIEN CLOTHES... MAKES SENSE.
I DON'T WANT TO FIGHT.
OH. YOU.
THE FIRST SLAYER. ARE YOU MAD AT ME--?
AGAIN...?

MUHN.
TU.
OUR TRIBES?
OUR... FAMILIES.
SO THIS INTERVENTION IS TO REMIND ME--WHAT?
EACH OF US IS ALONE...

"...BUT WE'RE A PART OF A WHOLE...
FOR RENT
"...SLAYER TO SLAYER IN A LONG LINE...
"...BUT I HAVE MY *OWN* WHOLE--THAT DIDN'T COME OUT RIGHT--I MEAN, I HAVE MY OWN TRIBE...
"...AN EXTENDED FAMILY THAT FIGHTS TOGETHER...
"...AND NEVER TURNS ITS BACK ON EACH OTHER..."
PARTY WENT DOWN HERE! CHEEZ-WHIZ AND HAND-GRENADES.
I LET HER DOWN, *ANGEL*.
WHO, BUFFY? YOU WERE IN *JAIL*, *FAITH*.
THERE WAS NOTHING YOU COULD'VE DONE.

THAT'S THE POINT-- I'M A SLAYER!
I KNOW WHY I WENT TO PRISON--THE THINGS I HAVE TO MAKE UP FOR--
--BUT I CAN'T HELP FEELING I COULD BE DOING SO MUCH MORE TO MAKE A DIFFERENCE ON THE OUTSIDE!
THAT'S WHAT SHE DOES TO US, ISN'T IT?
MAKES US BELIEVE WE CAN BE BETTER...?
NO.
GETS PRETTY FRUSTRATING, DON'T IT?
IS IT OKAY IF I FEEL BAD ABOUT THIS INSTEAD?
THE SCOURGE?!
KNOW 'EM, HUH?
YUP.
BAD?
DEFINE "BAD."
BAD CAN KICK MY ASS. ANYTHING ELSE --NOT SO BAD.
THEN IN THAT CASE, THEY MAKE BAD LOOK LIKE TELETUBBIES.

"...THAT'S THE KIND OF IMAGE THAT STAYS IN YOUR HEAD..."
OKAY, NICE TRY, BUT BEEN THERE AND DONE THAT--
--AND THIS IS NOT THE "LIGHT AT THE END OF THE TUNNEL."
NOT HEAVEN, THANK YOU.
SINCE YOU OBVIOUSLY WANT ME TO DIVE INTO THE DEEP END OF MY BRAIN...
...I'LL PLAY ALONG.
BUT JUST DON'T MAKE ME GO BACK TO VEGAS!
OKAY...DON'T KNOW YOU--OR YOU--OR YOU.
I THINK YOU HOOKED ME UP TO THE WRONG PARTY LINE.
IS THIS THE SUMMERS FAMILY REUNION?
NO. COULDN'T BE. YOU'RE ALL TOO HAPPY.
OF COURSE, THERE WAS MY DAD'S UNCLE MORRIS.
BUT HIS HAPPY WAS PHARMACEUTICAL, SO HE DOESN'T COUNT.

UHM... 'SCUSE ME--
PARDON ME--
--I DON'T DEAL TOO WELL WITH CROWDS...
...uhm... SLAYER AND ALL--GET ALL GRARR --STAKES--
--GET ANTSY WHEN I'M SURROUNDED BY--
--uhm-- VERY, VERY--
--VERY--
--HAPPY--
--PEOPLE...
uhm... WHAT--?
THANK...
...YOU...

WELCOME BACK.
I NEVER REALLY WENT ANYWHERE.
DIDN'T YOU?
WELL, IF YOU MEAN TO THE "ANGRY PLACE," THEN I GUESS I DID...
YOU GUYS WANTED ME TO CHILL, HUH?
WE ALL LEARN-- SOONER OR LATER--WHILE WE'RE ALIVE OR AFTER WE'RE DEAD...
...WE ALL LEARN IT'S NOT ABOUT SLAYING--
--IT'S ABOUT SAVING...

...SAVING...
AND IT TALKS.
WELCOME BACK.
SORRY ABOUT THAT. BUSINESS MEETING GOING ON IN MY HEAD.
HMM.
SO--?
WHOEVER IS BEHIND THIS PUSHED ME ON PURPOSE--
--LIKE THEY WANTED ME TO GO RAMBO AND LOSE CONTROL.
I DON'T KNOW WHY, BUT IT DIDN'T WORK--
--WELL, IT DID WORK, BUT I'M BETTER NOW.
AND YOU'RE GOING BACK THERE TO FIND OUT WHO DID IT.
YEAH. BUT YOU KNEW THAT ALREADY, HUH?
I HAVE NO CHOICE, PIKE. IT'S WHO I AM. WHAT I DO. AND MOST OF ALL...

"...MY FAMILY NEEDS ME."
AT LEAST NOW WE KNOW WHAT THE *PIPELINE* IS.
SPICY HUMANS GO IN, BLACK-MARKET DRUGS COME OUT.
GUYS-- WHAT DO WE DO?
I EXPECT WRITHE ABOUT IN HORRIFYING PAIN UNTIL WE EVENTUALLY *DROWN* OR PERHAPS *BOIL* TO DEATH.
OH.
SEE, *LOVE* YOU, HONEY, BUT *NOT* THE ANSWER SHE WAS LOOKING FOR.
LOVE ME--?
YEEAAA

ANGEL!!
HI, SQUIRT.
HEY, STUD. YOU PUT ON WEIGHT, OR ARE YOU JUST GLAD TO SEE ME?
uhm... C) ALL OF THE ABOVE--?
THAT WAY.
STUD--?
NOT NOW, SWEETIE...

CLEAR AHEAD!
AND BEHIND. THIS IS WEIRD.
WHY HAVEN'T THEY CHASED US?
THERE'S YOUR ANSWER--
IT'S FALLING APART!
MORE LIKE ONE BIG TRAP--
--BUT IT WASN'T LIKE THIS BEFORE!
THE SCOURGE COULDN'T HAVE REBUILT THIS ENTIRE PLACE.
SO WHO COULD?
XANDER HARRIS. I AM DISAPPOINTED.
HAVE I CHANGED THAT MUCH...

...SINCE THE LAST TIME YOU SAW ME?

OOOH, MULTIPLE CHOICE. I NEVER WAS GOOD WITH THAT WHOLE STANDARDIZED TEST THING--
--'CEPT DID I MENTION HOW WELL I DID ON MY SAT'S--?
--BUT REALLY, THAT'S NOT IMPORTANT, LET'S LOOK AT WHAT WE HAVE HERE...
A) FIGHT ME AND YOU DIE.
OR B) GIVE ME YOUR WEAPON--
--TAKE ME THROUGH THE INITIATIVE TUNNELS TO THE SCOURGE'S LIFEFORCE-SUCKING MACHINE--
--HELP ME FREE MY FRIENDS--
--AND STOP YOUR SUPERIORS FROM KILLING ALL OF HUMANITY.
OR THE EVEN-ACCEPTABLE C) STAND ASIDE AND LET ME BY.

SNNFFFF
HUMAN.
SLAYER?
WELL, YES AND NO...
KEEP OUT! DANGER
GO AWAY!!

WHY DO
THEY ALWAYS
CHOOSE A)?

MMPH

EXCUSE ME, I NEED THIS FACE!
CHAK
BUT YOU WON'T NEED THIS *ARM*, WILL YOU?
SNAPT
AND YOU CERTAINLY WON'T NEED *THOSE*...
OOPA!

STAKE--?
OH--THANKS, PIKE, BUT IT'S A DEMON. THEY DON'T DO STAKES.
NOT SURE WHAT TYPE, THOUGH--SOMETHING GESHUNDHEIT, I THINK--
ANYWHICH WAY IS BAD NEWS, CONSIDERING THE FACT HE'S WEARING A UNIFORM--
--AND MOST DEMONS PLAY SOLO...
WHAT...?
BEEN GONE A WHILE, BUT I THOUGHT THE TITLE SAYS BUFFY, THE VAMPIRE SLAYER?
YOU SHOULD PRINT NEW BUSINESS CARDS.

INTO EVERY GENERATION, A SLAYER IS BORN.
ONE GIRL, IN ALL THE WORLD, A CHOSEN ONE.
ONE BORN WITH THE STRENGTH AND SKILL TO HUNT THE VAMPIRES.

HMM... WHADDYA KNOW, NOTHING ABOUT DEMONS--

"--MAYBE WE CAN JUST DITCH THE OTHERS..."
ANYONE SEE "BUTCH CASSIDY AND THE SUNDANCE KID"?
ACTUALLY, AT THE ZIEGFELD WHEN IT FIRST CAME OUT.
UHM... FAITH-- ANGEL--FOR THE SAKE OF THOSE OF US WHO HAVEN'T BEEN BITTEN BY A RADIOACTIVE SPIDER--
--CAN YOU TWO BE A BIT MORE... RESPECTFUL?
XANDER IS RIGHT!
MY VENGEANCE ACCOUNTANT ALWAYS SAID, "YOU CAN CATCH MORE FLIES WITH EXPOSED INTESTINES THAN SPLATTERED BRAIN MATTER."
AND THANK YOU, ANYA, FOR THAT EXCERPT FROM MARTHA STEWART'S DEMON QUOTE BOOK...
IF MY SISTER WERE HERE, SHE'D KICK YOUR BUTTS IN--AGAIN!

THE CAPACITY FOR HUMANS TO REBEL AGAINST *ORDER* NEVER CEASES TO... AMUSE ME...
BUT YOUR SISTER WILL NOT SAVE YOU THIS DAY.
WE HAVE PLANNED THIS OPERATION TOO WELL.

WHEN I FIRST FOUND THE SCOURGE, I ADMIRED THEIR ADHERENCE TO STRUCTURE AND ORDER--
--YET THEY WERE SO LACKING IN... VISION.
THEIR PROGRAM--OR POGROM, IF YOU WILL--OF SPECIES SEARING IS A LIMITING ONE--
--WHICH, UPON ITS INEVITABLE COMPLETION, LEAVES LITTLE TO WHILE AWAY THEIR DAYS.
BUT THE OLD RACES WOULD HAVE TO STEP ASIDE FIRST--
--AND CONQUERING HUMANITY WOULD HAVE CAUSED UNNECESSARY... DECIMATION.
IT LACKS THE "GRINDING UNDER BOOTHEELS" MODEL PREFERRED BY MY ALLIES--

TAKING THE SOULS OF UNBORN CHILDREN AND TURNING THEM INTO A HIGHLY ADDICTIVE DRUG IS WHAT, A *HOBBY* FOR THEM?
ANY SOULS WILL SUFFICE. THAT UNBORN CHILDREN RUMOR WAS JUST... GOOD *MARKETING*.
WE WANTED TO STIMULATE INTEREST. HUMANS WHO HAVE SUCH INCLINATIONS PREFER THEIR SINS AS DEBASED AS POSSIBLE.
WHAT WOULD YOU KNOW ABOUT HUMANS, YOU'RE A TALKING LIGHTBULB!
MOTHER-- *DR. WALSH* --CREATED ME AS THE FIRST IN A NEW RACE OF HUMANS AND DEMONS.
SO YOU BUILT THE *PIPELINE* TO CREATE THE *SOUL DROPS*--
AND THEN SIT BACK AND LET MANKIND CONQUER *ITSELF*?
--YET ITS ELEGANCE MAKES UP FOR ITS DRAMATIC DEFICIENCIES.
THEN WHY BOTHER WITH THIS ARENA?
THE SCOURGE REQUIRE A *DIVERSION*. AND I REQUIRED A *POWER SOURCE*. IT SEEMED A LOGICAL SOLUTION.

THAT'S NOT LOGICAL, IT'S DUMB!
IXNAY ON THE UMBDAY.
NO, LOOK AT HIM--ADAM'S NOT EVEN REAL ANYMORE--HE'S DEAD!
I AM... UPGRADED... A MODIFIED PROGRAM --OF MY FORMER SELF.
THIS HOLOGRAPHIC FORM IS FOR THE BENEFIT OF YOUR LIMITED PERCEPTION. I TRANSCEND THE BOUNDARIES OF LIVING FLESH.
I AM A GHOST IN THE MACHINE-- AN ELECTROMAGNETIC FORCE OF NATURE--
--I AM... INDESTRUCTIBLE.
RECALL HEARING THOSE WORDS COME OUT OF YOUR MOUTH ONCE BEFORE, BIG A--
--ALSO RECALL THE WORD "UGHH"-- COMING OUT WHEN BUFFY RIPPED YOUR BIG C!
UHM --I JUST SAID ALL THAT OUT LOUD, DIDN'T I--?
DON'T WORRY, NO ONE GOT THE JOKE.
THE SLAYER MANAGED TO REMOVE MY URANIUM BATTERY BECAUSE SHE HAD ALSO BEEN... REPROGRAMMED --TEMPORARILY UPGRADED.
MY CURRENT OPERATING STATUS WILL PREVENT A RECURRENCE OF SUCH EVENTS.
OR IT WOULD...

"...HAD THE SLAYER NOT CHOSEN TO RUN AWAY..."
?
SPIKE...?
I CAN ALMOST FEEL HIM...THIS IS THE CELL HE WAS LOCKED IN.
HE'S BEEN GONE FOR WEEKS...
...GOOD RIDDANCE...

WHOA--
NO--I MEANT--I WAS MUMBLING...
...I HAVE A LOT OF HISTORY WITH THIS PLACE.
DEMONS GOT LOCKED UP AND KILLED HERE--
ALMOST LOST MY--A VERY GOOD FRIEND--HERE...
17

ONE SECOND YOU'RE MUTTERING YOU *SENSE* ME, NEXT YOU'RE POPPING MY HEAD LIKE A ZIT...
I'M FINE. AND I DIDN'T SAY *"PIKE,"* I SAID--
NEVER MIND...
WAIT, TWO YEARS AS A ROADIE FOR *MINISTRY,* YES--HEARING THAT BAD, NO--YOU DID *NOT* SAY, "NEVER MIND."
PLACE THIS BAD AND THEY DIDN'T LOCK UP AFTER THEY LEFT?
THEY WERE SUPPOSED TO *DROWN* IT IN *CONCRETE,* BUT IT *WAS* A GOVERNMENT CONTRACTING JOB...
...THEY MUST'VE CUT CORNERS--SHOCK THERE NOT?
THAT BIG ARENA I GOT YOU OUT OF WAS UP AHEAD.
THAT'S NOT WHERE I WANT TO GO--TOO MANY PEOPLE TO FIGHT THROUGH.
WE WANT TO SNEAK IN --SHUT DOWN THE MACHINE THEY HAVE KILLING PEOPLE.
BUT YOU DON'T EVEN KNOW IF THAT--
NEVER MIND.

OW
OW
OW
THE MAIN GENERATORS ARE DOWN HERE. THE INITIATIVE POWERED ITSELF BY INCINERATING ITS OWN WASTE AND RECYCLING ITS ENERGY.
IT'S THE ONLY PLACE THE SCOURGE COULD HAVE BUILT SOME-THING BIG ENOUGH TO PROCESS ALL THEIR PRISONERS.
UHM... SHOULD I EVEN ASK WHAT YOU MEAN BY "PROCESS"?
NO. HANG ON.
YOU SAID "INCINERATING" DIDN'T YOU?
WHICH, IMPLIES AN INCINERATOR...
WHICH BRINGS US TO --WHERE ARE THEY GETTING THE POWER THEY NEED TO RUN THIS PLACE?
UNLESS THEY TAPPED INTO TRUNK LINES OR AN OUTSIDE GENERATOR--
HEY, YEARS OF HANGING OUT WITH WILLOW ARE FINALLY PAYING OFF.
--SO THEIR ENERGY SOURCE HAS TO BE ON THE INSIDE SOME-HOW--DUH!--OF COURSE!
HERE WE GO...
...WHICH, BY THE WAY, INCINERATES THINGS...
PLEASE TELL ME YOU CAN FLY.

BUFFY!!
PIKE?
MAN, YOU GOT TALL!
BUT, BUFFY...

NO!!
INTERESTING. I RAN FOURTEEN HUNDRED POTENTIAL SCENARIOS AND THAT WASN'T ONE OF THEM.
BUFFY.
ADAM, WHAT IS HAPPENING?
I--I AM UNABLE TO EXTRAPOLATE THESE VARIABLES.
BLURP
LOOKS LIKE YOUR VARIABLES ARE ABOUT TO GET FLUSHED.

WE'RE LOSING ALL OF THE SOUL ENERGY!
I REALLY HATE HER.
SO YOU'RE THINKING, "WELL, THAT SUCKED."
WAIT 'TIL YOU SEE WHAT'S *NEXT*...

IS NOW THE PART WHERE I GET TO KICK SOME ASS?
NOW IS THE PART WHERE YOU GET TO KICK SOME ASS.
MY FAVORITE PART.
YOU HAVE STOPPED THE PIPELINE, DELAYED THE SCOURGE PERHAPS, BUT YOU CAN NOT DEFEAT ME.
AS LONG AS THE MEAT DOES WHAT IS SO PREDICTABLY EXPECTED OF THEM, I CAN NOT BE STOPPED.
YEAH, SEE, THAT WHOLE LACK OF-RESPECT FOR-OUR-INTELLIGENCE THING WOULD BE WHAT YOU WOULD CALL A "LOGIC FLAW."

SO THANKS FOR BABBLING
BUT I KINDA
FIGURED OUT
YOUR WEAKNESS ALREADY.
IT IS NOT A WEAKNESS, SINCE THE FLESH WILL ACT AS EXPECTED.
DON'T TELL ME, YOU DID THE MATH?
THE STATISTICAL PROBABILITY OF ANYONE CONVINCING THEM TO ACT OTHER-WISE IS--
NUMBERS. FOGGY. LET'S SEE HOW THINGS WORK IN REAL LIFE, WHY DON'T WE?
Uhm--HI. HELLO. REMEMBER ME? HERE'S THE DEAL, REAL SIMPLE.
THE SCOURGE ARE USING YOU! BY KEEPING ALL OF US FIGHTING CONSTANTLY--
--THEY'VE BEEN ABSORBING ALL THE ANGER AND FEAR GENERATED BY THE VIOLENCE AND CHANNELING IT TO POWER THIS PLACE--
--AND TO KEEP ADAM'S PROGRAM RUNNING!

AND ONCE YOU'RE TOO EXHAUSTED TO FIGHT ANYMORE, THEY MARCH YOU BEHIND THESE DOORS AND EXTERMINATE YOU!
AND YOU WANNA HEAR FLOGGING A DEAD HORSE? THEY USE YOUR SOULS TO CREATE A DRUG THAT'LL HELP THEM CONQUER MORE PEOPLE!
YOU ALL THOUGHT YOU HAD TO FIGHT FOR SURVIVAL, BUT THE TRUTH IS YOU'VE BEEN FIGHTING FOR THEIR SURVIVAL!
ALL WE HAVE TO DO TO WIN... IS STOP FIGHTING!
TOLD YOU. DIDN'T HAVE TO LIFT A FINGER.
NO--IF OUR POWER SOURCE DOES NOT MAINTAIN A CONSTANT CHARGE...
THE ENERGIZER BUNNY KEELS OVER...
"AND IT'S LIGHTS OUT!"
ZZZZZZMMMMMMMMMM

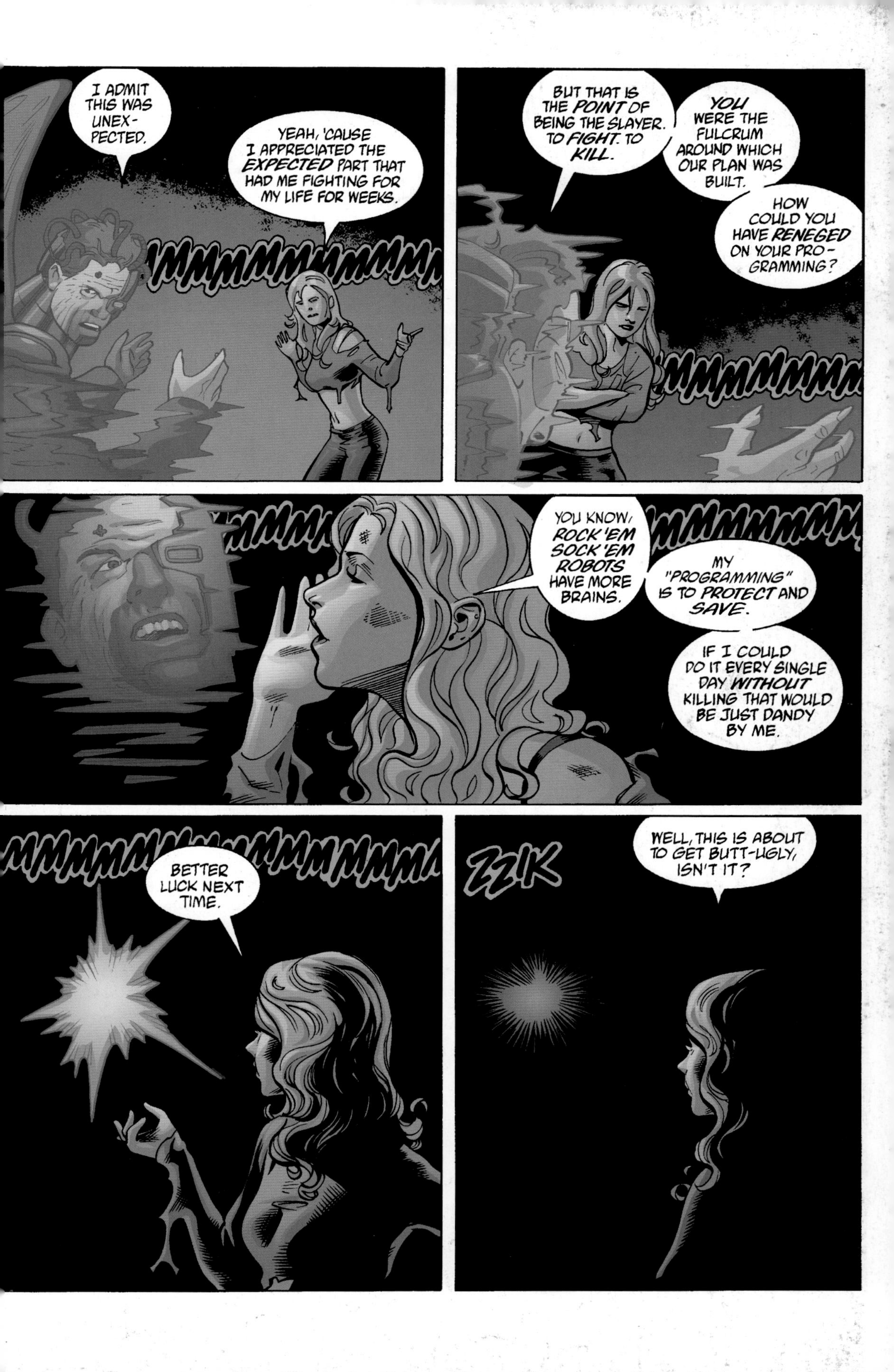
I ADMIT THIS WAS UNEX-PECTED.
YEAH, 'CAUSE I APPRECIATED THE EXPECTED PART THAT HAD ME FIGHTING FOR MY LIFE FOR WEEKS.
MMMMMMMMMMMMM
BUT THAT IS THE POINT OF BEING THE SLAYER. TO FIGHT. TO KILL.
YOU WERE THE FULCRUM AROUND WHICH OUR PLAN WAS BUILT.
HOW COULD YOU HAVE RENEGED ON YOUR PRO-GRAMMING?
MMMMMMMMM
YOU KNOW, ROCK 'EM SOCK 'EM ROBOTS HAVE MORE BRAINS.
MY "PROGRAMMING" IS TO PROTECT AND SAVE.
IF I COULD DO IT EVERY SINGLE DAY WITHOUT KILLING THAT WOULD BE JUST DANDY BY ME.
BETTER LUCK NEXT TIME.
ZZIK
WELL, THIS IS ABOUT TO GET BUTT-UGLY, ISN'T IT?

SO YOU KNEW THE PIPELINE WOULDN'T MELT YOU?
BUILT SLAYER TOUGH. SOMETIMES, I FORGET THAT.
HOME, SWEET HOME!
WHICH... THE SCOURGE WRECKED WHEN THEY ATTACKED US. FORGOT ABOUT THAT.
WELL, WE GOT A MESSY HOUSE, THEY GOT KILLED. FAIR EXCHANGE.
THEY COULD HAVE SHOWN SOME COMMON COURTESY AND LET YOU CLEAN UP THE DINNER PLATES FIRST.
YEAH, YOU'LL NEED THREE CEMENT TRUCKS.
NO, THE CEMENT IS THERE. GOVERNMENT CONTRACTORS NEVER POURED IT. YEAH, JUST FILL IT ALL IN.
SO THAT'S WHAT I BEEN MISSING OUT ON ALL THESE YEARS?
ONLY HALF.

THE FOOD IS TALKING BACK TO ME AND YOU DON'T HAVE ANY BEER.
CAN WE GET TEN PIZZAS AND FORTY POUNDS OF CHICKEN LO MEIN DELIVERED BEFORE I HAVE TO GO BACK TO PRISON?
SERIOUSLY, FAITH AND I WERE JUST GOOD FRIENDS.
WHO SORT OF DID IT.
ONCE.
AND SHE TRIED TO KILL ME AFTER-WARDS.
I KNOW THE FEELING.
NO, REALLY, I HAVE A SON AND HE'S YOUR AGE.
IS HE CUTE?
LISTENING?
YEAH.
THAT'S THE HALF YOU REALLY MISSED...

LATER...
FAITH, NEXT TIME I SEE YOU, I HOPE YOU HAVE NOWHERE ELSE TO GO.
SOON, B. YOU JUST WATCH YOUR BACK.
A SON, HUH?
YEAH.
KID'LL BE THE DEATH OF ME YET.
BUFFY--IT WAS PLANNED --I--SHE DIDN'T MEAN--I'M--
LIVING, ANGEL. IT'S WHAT WE'RE ALL DOING.
TAKE CARE OF YOURSEL OKAY?
YOU, TOO.
SO--?
PIKE WAS GOING TO TELL US ABOUT YOUR ROOKIE SEASON.
HEARD YOU WERE ALL BAT, BUT NO GLOVE.
DOES ANYONE GET YOUR JOKES?
Uh-uh. WE DO NOT HAVE TO DO A&E "BIOGRAPHY."
NO.
PLEASE.
...
JUST DON'T TALK ABOUT VEGAS.
FAIR ENOUGH.
SO WE'RE IN VEGAS, RIGHT, AND SHE'S A COAT-CHECK GIRL AT THIS CASINO WEARING A SKIRT UP TO HERE...
THE END

THE FIRST TIME

story FABIAN NICIEZA

illustrations PAUL LEE

This story takes place during Buffy the Vampire Slayer's seventh season.

MALL RATS

story and art ANDI WATSON

This story takes place during Buffy the Vampire Slayer's second season.

DARK HORSE COMICS®

The First Time

Fabian Nicieza
Illustrations by Paul Lee

"Excuse me?" Buffy said, with an extended drawl. Rarely, but sometimes, Dawn heard the long-dormant Valley Girl sneak out of her older sister. They sat across from each other in a booth at the Lick-It Ice Cream Shop. Dawn was devouring a Peanut Hot Fudge Blockbuster, taking scoops from Buffy's ChocoSludge when her sister wasn't looking. Surviving weeks of battle in the Scourge Arenas of Doom had significantly upped the "let's pig-out" factor in Dawn, whose High School metabolism normally burned at coal-furnace levels anyway.

"Your first time," Dawn said. "Your first vamp."

"Oh."

"What did you—*oh, no*—thank you very much for the Skinemax brain-flash," Dawn said, shivering as punctuation. "Just, what with you training me, I was wondering how it was for you when you first started."

Buffy stared out the window at daytime Sunnydale. Everyone going about their business, usually so oblivious, or so grateful, that they had survived another day. And there was Buffy, with the responsibility of keeping them alive on her shoulders.

"My first vamp," Buffy repeated, crinkling her nose, weighing the memory. Wondering if it was a recollection worth the price of guilt.

"You don't remember?" asked Dawn.

❧

The tombstone had read:

Robert Berman
God Is At His Heels

It was dark. She was scared. She didn't believe any of it. The strange man named Merrick stood by her side. With a stake and cross in hand.

He was her first Watcher, for all of the few weeks that had lasted. He had brought her to the cemetery to make her accept the truth about her destiny. To make her believe she was the Chosen One.

Buffy had only come here to get this guy off her back.

By comparison, he made "creepy" look positively Rodeo Drive. And he talked like a bad TV late-night horror-film host. And all of that was made moot the second Robbie Berman's decomposed hand ripped out from the ground. Followed by the rest of Robbie. Including the fangs.

Her first thought had been, *Nice suit. Those grass stains will never come out.*

Her second thought involved unintelligible half-syllables that bounced off each other in exaggerated slow motion like a primitive game of Pong.

Merrick pushed her aside and engaged Robbie Berman. A second vamp ripped through the ground and grabbed Buffy's ankles. Instinct and self-preservation kicked in. She smacked the woman in the head with the cross.

As the vamp squealed, Buffy eye-rolled major annoyance that two vampires had risen from graves in such close proximity. Weren't there city ordinances for that kind of thing?

Buffy turned to see Merrick getting his butt handed to him by Robbie Berman. She hesitated, then stake in hand, she leapt towards the vampire, putting aside the sheer ick-factor of what she was about to do. She prepared herself for the sound of wood piercing flesh. And muscle. And bone. She prepared herself for the thought of ending someone's life (*granted, an undead monster-life, but still...*).

She prepared for all of this in a fraction of a second.

And then she missed!

The stake glanced off Robbie's shoulder nearly poking Merrick's eye out. The Watcher maintained his composure and rolled Robbie off of him. The newborn vampire's momentum carried him towards Buffy, knocking her backwards. He fell on top of her. She felt a flash of resistance. Then a shove as skin gave way.

And just like that, Robbie Berman turned to dust.

He had accidentally fallen on top of her stake.

Before Buffy could even gather herself, a high-pitched growl ripped through the air as the woman-vamp dove towards her. Buffy spun at her wail, scared, oblivious to the fact she was still holding the stake in her hand. The vampire missed her, landing on the grass with a thud. As she stood over the surprised creature, a thought flashed through Buffy's mind: *When did I get so fast?*

Merrick shoved his way past her and dug his stake into the woman's chest. Buffy watched the cloud of ash from the vampire's dusting settle over her shoes and the cuffs of her pants. She tried to reconcile the audacity of the last three minutes. It was absurd enough to be laughable. So why wasn't she laughing? Vampires? *Check.* Killed vampires? *Check.* Stained your Gucci half-pumps and pressed Armani linen pants with the sooty remains of aforementioned vamps? *Check.*

She didn't say anything. She didn't know what to say.

She felt a hand on her shoulder. It wasn't meant to be comforting, just guiding her, out and away from the cemetery.

When they reached her house, Merrick said, "Now get some sleep, Slayer."

As if.

Everyone in the house was asleep. She went on her mom's computer and looked up information on Robert Berman. It took her a while to figure how to navigate the search engine, but she showed unusual patience. Maybe born of exhaustion?

Or guilt.

She found his date of birth. His address. His obituary.

His High School web-site profile. She went on message boards he'd visited. Postings on different *X-Files* boards. Comic book boards. RPG sites. He'd been a geek by her standards.

By her standards, she thought. She was categorizing a dead teenager.

Here he was, nothing more or less than what he'd been: a decent kid who got decent grades and lived a decent life.

He didn't deserve to be killed by vampires (*as if anyone did*).

He didn't deserve to get killed…by her.

Buffy clutched her stomach, reaching for a garbage can under the desk. She threw up. Her pain was about more than just Robert, although that played a hefty part in the jag. It included her concerns about her parents' obvious and mounting problems to Buffy's own secret (*and mounting*) disgust with herself every single time she looked in the mirror.

For so long, she'd put people into pre-arranged slots: geeks, ginkers, jocks, dolls, studs, etc. As if it were perfectly acceptable for human beings to be sorted like mail.

She wanted to be a better person than that. She needed to be a better person.

And having survived this night, on the long, hollow walk home from the cemetery, she had wondered if this was her chance to be more than she ever thought she would be…could be? But by becoming this mythical warrior Chosen One, would she have to lose her humanity to the Slayer? She didn't know if she could be both, a caring, helping person and a monster-killing machine.

She didn't know if she had the strength to find out.

That's when Buffy had started to cry. And she kept on crying until she had cried herself to sleep.

A nudge on her shoulder woke her up two hours later. She looked up, groggy, her mouth tasting like old rubber. Dawn leaned over her, pajamas on, fuzzy pink slippers tickling Buffy's fingers. Buffy noticed her younger sister had snatched Mr. Gordo again. Eight-year-old klepto, she thought.

"I had to pee," said Dawn. "Uhm… you okay?"

"Just fell asleep," muttered Buffy, standing up.

Dawn looked at the computer screen. "What's this?" she asked.

Buffy cursed her Mom for never programming the screen saver. She quickly closed out of the different files she'd left open.

"Let's go to bed," Buffy said.

"Was that your boyfriend?" asked Dawn.

Surprising herself, Buffy suppressed a giggle at the thought she'd ever have a vampire for a boyfriend. Then she stopped at the door to her Mom and Dad's study and stared at the blank screen. What *was* Robert Berman exactly? Was he a monster who needed to be killed or the boy who had become a vampire? She understood that if this whole Slayer thing *were* going to happen, she'd better learn to separate the life a person lived before becoming a vampire with what they were afterwards.

"He was nobody…," she said, and whispered a silent apology as the words left her lips.

They walked upstairs. When Buffy finally fell asleep again, the nightmares came calling…and her new life was just beginning…

❧

Dawn's spoon clinked against the side of her sundae glass. The sound snapped Buffy out of her reverie. "Did you say something?" she asked.

"Said I was just surprised is all," Dawn said, finishing her sundae with several borderline-maniacal tongue-wipes of the spoon, a lion on the veldt licking its paws clean of the kill. "About you not remembering."

"Why?" asked Buffy.

"I just guess I would," Dawn replied. "I mean, yeah, by now, routine and all, but back then, your very first one?"

Buffy stared out the window for a moment. She had adopted a pretty hard shell about the matter after that first night. She knew if she hadn't, it would have hurt too much to be the Slayer. *More than usual*, she mused.

She looked at Dawn out of the corner of her eye, her little sister getting so big, trying to sneak another spoonful of Buffy's shake. She wondered how much her sister should think about such things.

Buffy clicked her teeth quickly, nervously, for a few seconds. Then she turned and faced Dawn, smacking her hand gently. She snipped, "Stop stealing my ChocoSludge."

"Busted," Dawn said. They giggled and then silence hung between them.

"His name was Robert Berman," Buffy blurted out.

"Huh?"

"The first one. Robert Berman."

"Oh," said Dawn.

Buffy could tell that had satisfied Dawn's curiosity, but she didn't want to stop now. "He was a freshman at UCLA. I think Xander would have liked him," she continued. "He was a big *X-Files* fan. A little awkward with girls. Not too many friends, I think. He was a film student and he had a younger sister who won a science contest and…"

"Wait," interrupted Dawn.

"What?"

"Is it a long story?"

"You mind?"

"No, not at all," Dawn said, pushing her empty sundae glass to the side of the table. "I just think I'll need another one of these."

They ordered a second round of frozen fat. Dawn listened as her sister told the story of a vampire's death and a young man's life.

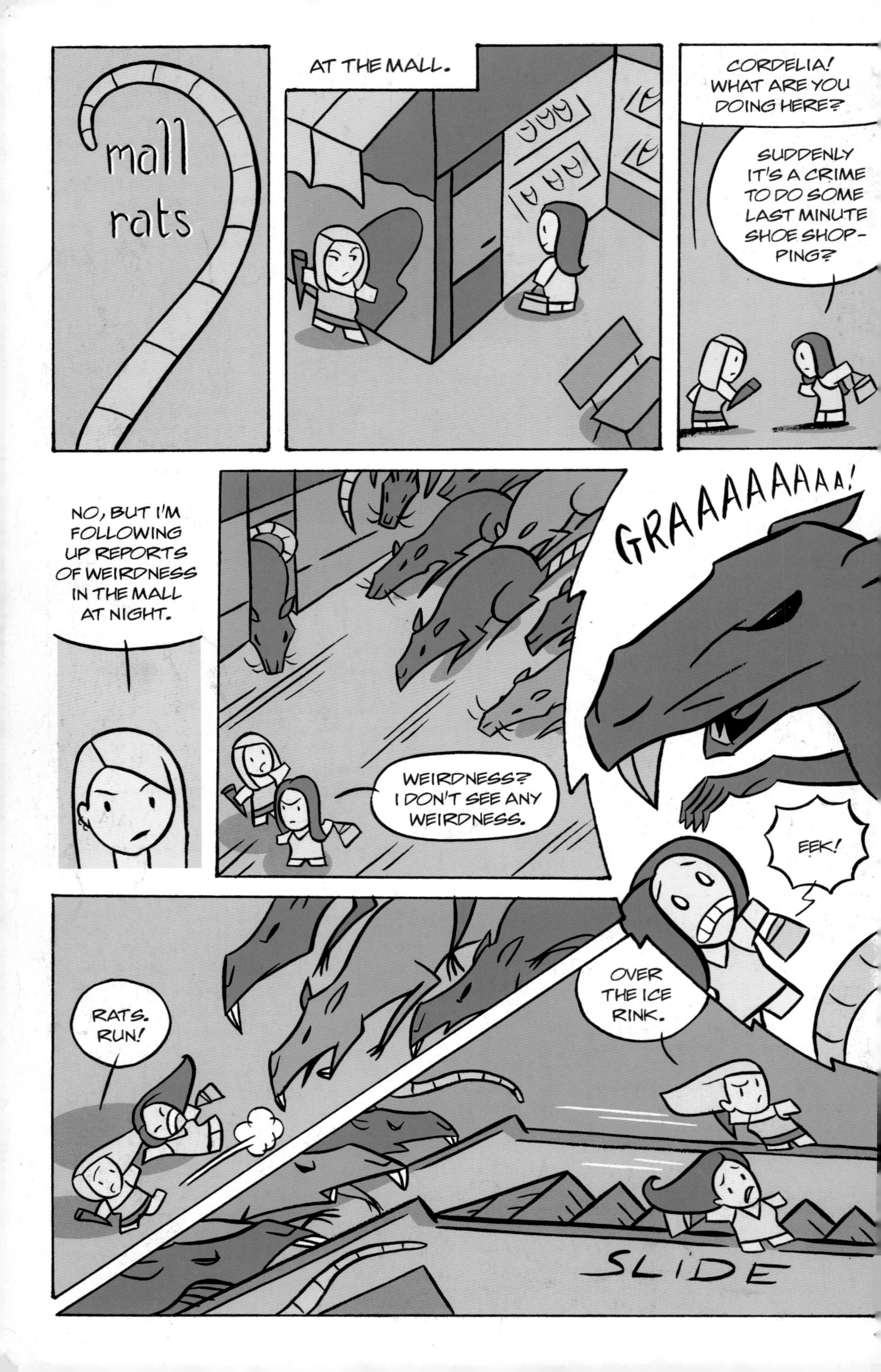
mall rats
AT THE MALL.
CORDELIA! WHAT ARE YOU DOING HERE?
SUDDENLY IT'S A CRIME TO DO SOME LAST MINUTE SHOE SHOP-PING?
NO, BUT I'M FOLLOWING UP REPORTS OF WEIRDNESS IN THE MALL AT NIGHT.
WEIRDNESS? I DON'T SEE ANY WEIRDNESS.
GRAAAAAAAA!
EEK!
RATS. RUN!
OVER THE ICE RINK.
SLIDE

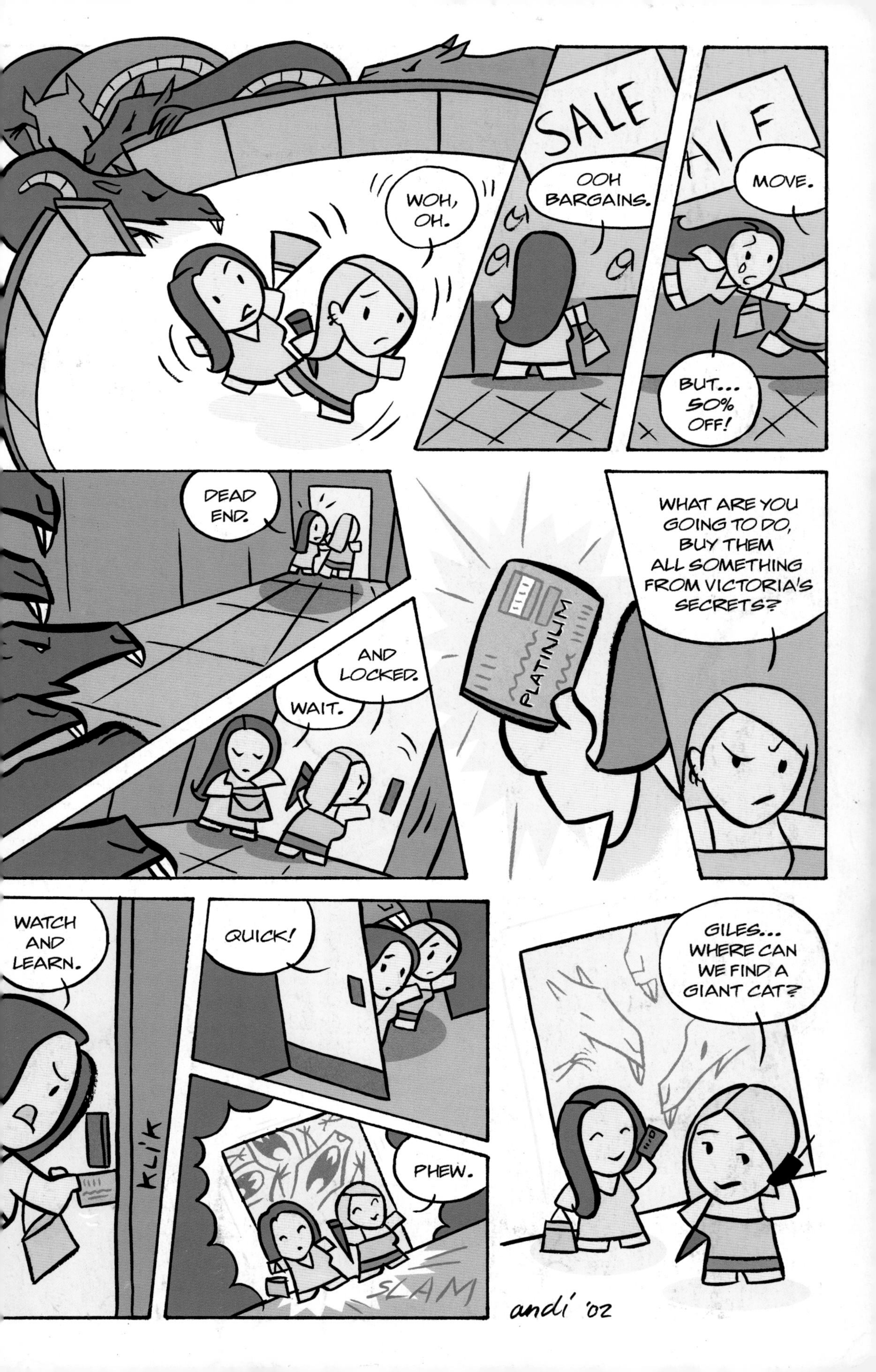
WOH, OH.
SALE
OOH BARGAINS.
MOVE.
BUT... 50% OFF!
DEAD END.
AND LOCKED.
WAIT.
PLATINUM
WHAT ARE YOU GOING TO DO, BUY THEM ALL SOMETHING FROM VICTORIA'S SECRETS?
WATCH AND LEARN.
KLIK
QUICK!
PHEW.
SLAM
GILES... WHERE CAN WE FIND A GIANT CAT?
andi '02

PAUL LEE and BRIAN HORTON